CARDS OF CAMELOT

A 54-Card Deck and Rule Book

Cards of Camelot: A 54-Card Deck and Rule Book
copyright © 2024 by Magnolia Porter Siddell and Ver. All rights
reserved. Printed in China. No part of this book may be used or
reproduced in any manner whatsoever without written permission
except in the case of reprints in the context of reviews.

Andrews McMeel Publishing
a division of Andrews McMeel Universal
1130 Walnut Street, Kansas City, Missouri 64106

www.andrewsmcmeel.com

24 25 26 27 28 RLP 10 9 8 7 6 5 4 3 2 1

ISBN: 978-1-5248-8606-6

Editor: Katie Gould
Designer: Tiffany Meairs
Production Editor: Brianna Westervelt
Production Manager: Jeff Preuss

ATTENTION: SCHOOLS AND BUSINESSES
Andrews McMeel books are available at quantity discounts with bulk
purchase for educational, business, or sales promotional use.
For information, please e-mail the Andrews McMeel Publishing
Special Sales Department: sales@amuniversal.com.

CARDS OF CAMELOT

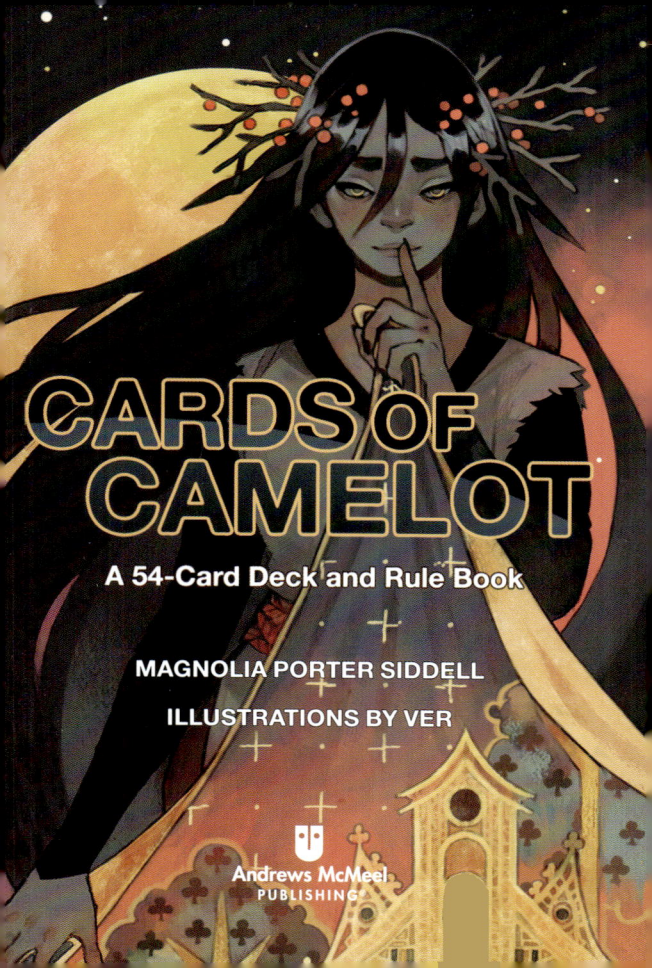

A 54-Card Deck and Rule Book

MAGNOLIA PORTER SIDDELL

ILLUSTRATIONS BY VER

Andrews McMeel
PUBLISHING

TABLE OF CONTENTS

INTRODUCTION . . . 1

INSTRUCTIONS . . . 3

◆

FACE CARDS STORIES . . . 5

MORGAUSE, QUEEN OF CLUBS . . . *6*

GAWAIN, KING OF CLUBS . . . *8*

HOLY GRAIL, ACE OF HEARTS . . . *10*

GALAHAD, JACK OF HEARTS . . . *12*

THE LADY OF THE LAKE, ACE OF DIAMONDS . . . *15*

LANCELOT, KING OF HEARTS . . . *17*

MERLIN, KING OF DIAMONDS . . . *19*

GUINEVERE, QUEEN OF HEARTS . . . *22*

MORGAN LE FAY, ACE OF CLUBS . . . *25*

ARTHUR, KING OF SPADES . . . *28*

ELAINE, QUEEN OF DIAMONDS . . . *31*

MORDRED, JACK OF SPADES . . . *34*

IGRAINE, QUEEN OF SPADES . . . *37*

AGRAVAIN, JACK OF CLUBS . . . *40*

UTHER PENDRAGON, ACE OF SPADES . . . *42*

YVAIN, JACK OF DIAMONDS . . . *45*

✦
CARD GAMES . . . 47
ALUETTE . . . *48*

KARNÖFFEL . . . *52*

CARTOMANCY . . . *56*

✦

CONCLUSION . . . 63

ACKNOWLEDGMENTS . . . 64

BIBLIOGRAPHY & FURTHER READING . . . 65

✦

REX QUONDAM REXQUE FUTURUS

INTRODUCTION

✦

Of all the stories in the Western world, those of King Arthur and the men and women who loved him have a strange power even today, unexplainable even to me. No matter where I go, I find echoes of these stories everywhere, woven into unimaginable details, places, people, time itself. Even if you have never read a word about King Arthur, you are likely to know his name, and even the names of his companions. When you first hear his stories, they may ring with familiarity, echoing as they do through thousands of stories told throughout time.

It was I who said that Arthur, who was king once, would be king again, but the older I get, the more I wonder at the real meaning of such a prophecy. Do I really believe that Arthur, my old friend, will walk the Earth again as I do?

To be honest, the man I knew was nothing like the stories they tell today, yet there is a piece of him in all of them. Perhaps, the more you read of him, the more complete a picture you might hold of him in your mind. Of course, I knew him hundreds of years ago. The memories I have drift in and out of my mind like scraps of a dream. If you read enough about King Arthur, you may know him even better than I do.

I wonder if that is the meaning of the prophecy that Arthur will be king again. Even in this strange and unprecedented new year, he is still the king in so many minds. Perhaps he always will be, and in that way, he might live forever.

The stories you hold here in your hands accompany a deck of cards, which you can use for games and for magic—two of my favorite things to share with Arthur, that I now share with you. Thank you, dear reader, for helping me keep him alive. —Merlin

INSTRUCTIONS

✦

Dear reader, you now hold in your hands a very special deck of cards. Each of the face cards—the Kings, Queens, Jacks, and Aces—depict a figure from the everlasting tales of King Arthur. You can read this rule book for more stories and games to play, including some games that Arthur and his knights might have played in the days of Camelot.

What's more, if a clever hand were to place the cards in the order in which the stories are told, the connections between these figures will be revealed in the art. After all, even King Arthur is nothing without his Round Table, his family, and the witches and wizards who have played their parts in his story, and so these cards are intertwined.

You, too, have a part in King Arthur's legend, for a story is nothing without someone to hear it, to imagine it, and to carry it into the future. So, read the stories, play the games, and help illuminate these tales. Keep these cards in your pocket wherever you go, for you never know when you might need them. And of course, you can always use them to play any card game you like.

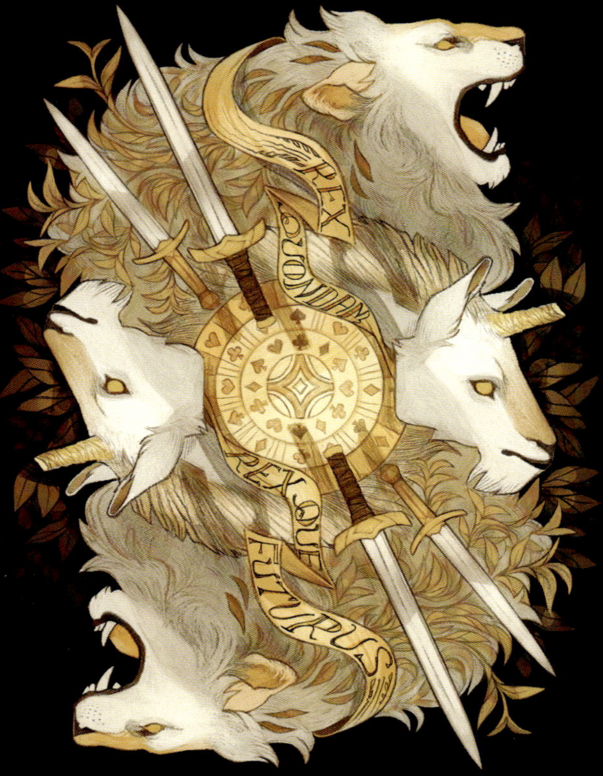
REX
QUONDAM
REX QUE
FUTURUS

FACE CARDS
STORIES
✦ ✦ ✦

MORGAUSE, QUEEN OF CLUBS

THE QUEEN OF FIRE

Morgause did everything for herself. That had always been so, and she was happy for it. What was the point of living for anyone else? She didn't worry about her sons. They were smart enough, and strong, and if they lived by her example, they would make their own satisfaction. And certainly no one else would do anything for her.

Her own mother never taught her the magic she knew. Morgause had to teach herself, hunched over the books by candlelight, burning herself on the wax.

Morgause lived in luxury as a queen. If her sisters had hoped to fare better, they certainly hadn't. They gave their lives for their children, for the kingdom, for the hand of fate—and where had it gotten them? Morgan, skin and bones, living in the woods like an animal. Igraine, dead and forgotten, even by her own son.

Morgause's mother, the Lady of the Lake, had set all this spinning, and for what purpose? What grand resolution? Kings lying bleeding on the floor. Marriages broken and trust shattered. A child so twisted by hate he could barely be called human.

She never knew what her mother had wanted. She'd never even known what she was thinking. The only heart that wasn't a mystery to her was her own. So she would follow it, and damn everything else.

At least by being selfish she only burned the ones who loved her. When you tried to help, it seemed, you set fire to the whole world.

GAWAIN, KING OF CLUBS

GAWAIN AND THE GREEN KNIGHT

Gawain struck off the Green Knight's head. To his shock, the Knight picked it up and put it back on. "Come to me in a year's time," he said. "And, as promised, I will deal you the same blow you have dealt me."

A year passed, and the whole court of Camelot begged Gawain not to go. He did not even know where the Green Knight's chapel lay. To quest for it, and find no treasure at the end but his own death?

But Gawain went. It was dishonorable to forget a promise, and cowardly to run from your own fate.

In his heart, deep down, he wondered. For honor, for courage . . . but was there another reason? His brothers were slain. His mother dishonored. The woman he had killed—the world had forgotten her, forgotten any reason not to praise him. But he still remembered that empty stare in her pale, open eyes.

He was a warrior, fearless, but the anger and pain inside him was something worse than a hunger for battle. It frightened him like a child when he lay awake at night.

Maybe he welcomed the blow from the Green Knight. Maybe, in the end, it was easier that way.

When the Knight's axe did nothing but nick his flesh, Gawain was flooded with relief. Not just for his life, but for the discovery that he *wanted* his life at all. The pain was still there, heavier than anything else he knew, but he would carry it, at least for one more day.

HOLY GRAIL, ACE OF HEARTS

THE QUEST FOR THE GRAIL

The Grail is waiting for you.
   Will you walk until your feet ache?
Will you search so long and far that the way home is lost forever?
Will you offer your face to the ones who hate you most and let them cut? How about your eyes? Your heart?

Are you sure you deserve the Grail?

Will you put aside the ones you love?
Will you let the sound of their voices slip from your mind?
Will you accept that if you see them again they will not know your face?
Will you let them die? Would you kill them yourself, if I ask? They could be sinners. They could be demons in disguise.

Are you tired? Do you hurt? Do you long for home? Do you need a kind word?

Do you really want the Grail?

You don't deserve it.
You don't deserve it.
You don't deserve it.

GALAHAD,
JACK OF HEARTS

THE SILENT KNIGHT

Galahad was always sweet and quiet. As a child, he did his chores and never complained. He never asked his mother for anything. She wished sometimes that he would. It was lonely to love someone who would not take anything from you.

He grew into a holy knight and, like his father Lancelot, had an impossible grace with a sword. By all accounts he was even greater than his famous father, who had stormy moods and a troubled heart. Galahad was clear and true as a bell.

A man named Percival was his companion, and their adventures together were many. Galahad could see demons in the hearts of men, and cast them out by sliding his spear softly through. His quiet smile never broke for the bodies left behind.

Percival was there when Galahad found the cracked and wasted King of the Desert. The old man had become a beggar, with a wound that bled out endlessly into the dust. Galahad could heal him with a blessed word, but Percival watched as he kept his smiling silence. He was a holy knight, but it was God's job to show mercy, not his.

It was on the quest for the Grail that Percival realized two things. The first was that the other knights were scared of Galahad. His radiance was too bright; they felt weak and wrong just being near him. The second was that they thought Percival was Galahad's closest friend. He was not sure he believed that, because being a friend meant understanding him, and Percival was never sure that he did.

It was Galahad who found the Grail. It was he, and only he, who was pure enough to lay hands on it. But when he touched the holy prize, he turned back toward his companions, just for a moment. His eyes were so wide. He opened his mouth, but before any sound could escape, his body crumpled and fell. They would not ever know what he was about to say.

The other knights said he had ascended to Heaven, shed his earthly body and returned to God. His face, they said, was filled with blazing joy. But Percival thought differently. To him, it was the face of an animal caught in the jaws of something larger. Or the face of a little boy who truly realized for the first time that he would die.

Percival hoped he was wrong. He hoped he really couldn't know Galahad's true feelings. But lying awake at night, he had the terrifying thought: maybe the two of them really were friends. Maybe he was the only one who understood.

THE LADY OF THE LAKE, ACE OF DIAMONDS

THE HAND BEHIND IT ALL

The Lady of the Lake bore three daughters—Igraine, Morgause, and at last, little Morgan (born at just the same moment as Igraine's son, Arthur).

Mortal men called that a coincidence, or an evil trick of luck, that the Witch should be born at the same moment as the King. But the Lady knew it had happened for one simple reason. She had wanted it to happen, so it did. Whatever they wanted to call it did not matter to her. She was a holy woman, and she knew the old gods.

The Lady was unsentimental. A holy woman does not bear children for her own pleasure. Each girl had been born for a purpose, and not all were happy ones.

She let them go astray, far away and apart, smiling sadly as they left, knowing she'd never see them again. They thought they had chosen their own ways. They even thought they were escaping her influence, as if such a thing were possible. Even Morgan, powerful as she became, was blind to it. Her daughters' feet could only ever follow the paths she had laid for them.

Though they seemed scattered across the world, you could draw a circle between them like points on a map, and at the center would be the pinpoint mark of fate.

It didn't matter if her daughters despised her, so long as that mark was drawn out.

That's what she told herself years after, lying sleepless in her cold bed.

LANCELOT, KING OF HEARTS

THE TALE OF SIR LANCELOT

Lancelot could cut anything with his sword. He even, unknown to others, sliced his own heart into pieces.

One piece for the King, for whom his adoration was as fierce as his betrayal.

One for the Queen, who he tried to forget till his head ached, but still drew her into himself each night, helplessly as air.

One for his God, who saw all of his sins in body and mind and received in return his most shameful desire.

How could he love the King and Queen so much without a whole heart to give them? How could he love his God? He had divided himself up until there was nothing left for anyone else—not even for himself. That the King and Queen loved him back was just another way he had tricked them, burdened them. That his God loved him back—well, he could never believe in that.

When the people saw his armor shine on the battlefield, they sang out his name. When they saw him win every tournament, with easy grace and a proud smile, they wept in adoration. He knew they couldn't see how small he was inside. To deceive them was just another of his daily cruelties.

No one knew that each swing of his sword was a prayer—that those pieces of him could someday be fixed and made whole. But no matter how great he was, he could never make a sword do anything but cut.

MERLIN, KING OF DIAMONDS

ONCE AND FUTURE

Merlin dreamed of the future and the past. His dreams were so vivid, they were another waking life. He watched friends die, and broke bread with their grandmothers the next night. When he was awake, it was hard to tell... Well, what was "awake"? What was "real"? He was a man of great magical power, but he was always a little boat, at the mercy of a storm.

Except when he was with Arthur, who was a beacon. When they spoke, he was anchored in one place and one time, and it gave him some peace.

But still, there were times when he touched the boy's hand, and felt the wrinkles of a man much older than himself. Or, when Arthur played wooden swords with Kay, Merlin saw the shadow of a real blade pierce his heart. Arthur, with his sweet hesitant voice, always asked him in those moments why he had suddenly started to cry.

The council of animals had taken a great interest in the boy. His life—and death—would ripple enormously throughout the world. The old wizard was happy to guide Arthur, to spend time with him, on their orders. Still, Merlin's blood was so rich with magic, there was nothing he touched that was not changed by it. Was Arthur really so special, or had he too been changed, just by virtue of being near Merlin? If he left Arthur alone, would he still be so wrapped up in his doomed fate? Would the sword in the stone still be there, waiting for another unlucky boy to yank it free, or would it even exist at all?

No, wait, Merlin reminded himself. That hadn't happened yet.

He could turn away right now and never see Arthur again. Maybe the boy would grow up to be Kay's humble squire, and never know that another future had once lain in wait for him. But still, Arthur was the lighthouse in the tumult of Merlin's dreams. And he, like all powerful wizards, was in the end a very selfish man.

GUINEVERE, QUEEN OF HEARTS

THE BETRAYAL OF THE QUEEN

Guinevere was a good queen. She knew that, and her King knew it. But if her people knew it, they never mentioned it.

Instead they whispered about how she never gave Arthur children, as if it was her choice, as if her wish for a child didn't ache in her bones.

They remembered every time she forgot to smile, and every time she smiled too much. They remembered how her face paint was too red—and at her age! They remembered the times, once or twice, when she let her white-hot anger spill for just a moment, and forgot her infinite success, day after day, at holding it in.

They called her frigid, a harlot, a shrew, a harpy. No matter what she did, no matter even if the names contradicted each other—they called her those things anyway.

It was all just a game to them, which they would always win and she would always lose. Who could blame them for enjoying a game that was rigged in their favor? Perhaps they had nothing else to look forward to. That, at least, was something she could understand.

But in that case, she thought, shouldn't she enjoy her own games? If they called her an adulteress either way... why not? Why not taste the pleasure Lancelot brought to her from the wild outside her walls? A stolen hour or two against a lifetime? A chance at real love— wasn't it a sin to let that slip away?

If it was a bad choice, at least it was one that was, for once, her own to make.

Let them have their fun. She would have hers. And even when she was a frail old woman, locked in a convent with her husband dead in the ground, she still couldn't bring herself to regret it.

MORGAN LE FAY, ACE OF CLUBS

MORGAN IN THE MISTS

She didn't know how the young couple had stumbled upon her. Her home in the woods was secluded, but somehow, the world always had a way of finding her again, no matter how much she tried to hide. Still, they were here, so Morgan thought to show them some courtesy. They sat down at her plain little wooden table, and she served them some tea.

It didn't take long for the rude and probing questions to start. For someone so feared as a witch, they didn't seem at all concerned about upsetting her. They were, she thought, almost sweet in their stupidity.

They asked her if she hated Arthur, or was she jealous of his greatness? Was she really born of the wicked faeries, or was she just a witch who had worked some evil spell? Or was it that she herself was a curse incarnate, wrought from the hidden world beyond, and like a black cat, she had brought that evil upon Arthur, simply by being near him?

How else to explain the ruin Camelot had come to?

She smiled a secret smile.

The love she held for sweet Arthur, all her life. The work she had given all her magic and strength to seeing done—for him, for his kingdom. The problem with magic was that it had consequences beyond what even she could see. Had it all come to wrong, or was the right she had worked for still slowly on its way? Either way, the truth was invisible to them. But it wasn't their fault. They were blind little mice who couldn't see beyond their whiskers.

They would never love her for the work she had done. But why should she care?

The cat, after all, doesn't wish for the love of the mouse.

When she said that out loud, they ran from her. It was fun, she had to admit, to keep them guessing.

ARTHUR, KING OF SPADES

THE HUNT FOR THE WHITE STAG

The stories all said that the White Stag would elude capture for eternity.

But King Arthur knew—even for a beast of magic—there was no escape from death.

When spring bloomed again, the Round Table all mounted their finest horses and went on a hunt for the Stag. Every year, they returned home empty-handed, but happy, with eyes pleasantly tired from sunshine and the trees' blazing green.

This was the part Arthur loved best. After the war, the blood, the death, the choices he had made—it had all been for days like this. All that pain, just for a moment, disappeared from his mind. He wasn't a king anymore. He was a man, riding with his friends, breathing the sweet air and laughing loudly without fear.

But there is no real escape, not even for a King.

He thought he knew that. Merlin taught him that when he was young. But the year he actually found the White Stag, he knew it more deeply than he ever had before.

The Stag was old, like him. He saw the broken antler and the catch in its step. Life had weakened it, and really, any hunter could have had it, in such a state. But of course, Arthur was the one to find it. Things always seemed to happen for him that way.

When he slew the White Stag, he wept. Not for the end of the legend, just for the life of a deer that would never again run in the forest.

He wondered if anyone would weep for the boy who ran through the trees when his lessons were done, waving the wooden sword his brother Kay had made for him, watching the birds in the trees and the fish in the river, who thought all animals were magic.

ELAINE, QUEEN OF DIAMONDS

THE QUESTING BEAST

When Elaine was a little girl, the people around her didn't hide how they felt about her father. "That idiot, Pellinore," they laughed, not caring that she could hear them.

"Does he really think he'll catch the Questing Beast? Does he really even think it exists?" Their voices took on a cruel mockery of her father's soft, warbling tone. "'A fiend with the body of a leopard, and the head of a serpent, and a voice like a hundred hounds braying!' If he expects us to believe him, he's stupider even than we thought!"

She asked him one day, crying. "Why do you do it? Why do you chase the Beast? Don't you know they all laugh at you?"

He smiled at her, and his gentle eyes twinkled. "Of course I know, my dear. But I also know my Beast is out there, and I can't let the laughter of some silly fools stop me from finding her, now can I?"

He dried her tears, and his mustache tickled her forehead when he kissed her. She couldn't help but giggle.

"That's my girl. We both know I'll find it, one of these days. We'll see who laughs at us then, eh?"

She loved him more than anything in that moment.

When she was grown, holding little Galahad in her arms, waiting by the window in her empty room, she tried her hardest to remember her father's words. Lancelot hadn't returned for his son. It had been months, almost a year now. Would he ever return? Would he ever love her the way she wanted? She knew their baby was special. Maybe, if she raised him well, he would grow up to be the best and most holy of all knights. Would that, at least, be enough reason for Lancelot to come back?

She remembered the kindly certainty in her father's eyes. The courage he had while chasing his silly dream. She had to hold on to her own dream, just like him, and know someday that it would come true.

She tried her hardest to believe that, she really did. But some days, the bad dreams—and the empty chill in her heart—were easier to believe in.

MORDRED,
JACK OF SPADES

THE DEATH OF ARTHUR

After it happened, even months later, it was all anyone could talk about. King Arthur killed, stabbed in the back by his own son, Mordred. The name even sounded like "murder"...

One soldier claimed to have met him.

"He didn't seem like a bad person. He was quiet at first, but when you got him talking, he wouldn't shut up. He fought with us for a little while, in his father's own army. Wasn't the strongest fighter, but he wasn't a coward either.

"He could paint, did you know that?" the soldier asked, though he knew his fellows were not as interested in the less gory details. "He painted the bird on my shield here. A goose. He got the feathers right and everything ... gray stripes, just like the geese on my mother's farm." There was a catch in the soldier's voice. "I didn't even tell him what kind of goose I wanted. It's like he just..."

"What's your point?" asked his friends. "You're saying he wasn't so bad? He killed his own father. Our King. And now he's dead, too."

"You should throw that shield away," said one man, in a quiet voice.

The soldier hesitated. He knew Mordred had believed his own father tried to drown him as a baby. But how could he remember something like that? There was no way to know if it was true, and even if it was, no one else would want to hear it.

Some people held on to their pain, like they'd die without it, and they never realized the opposite was true. The soldier had seen it more than once in his life. Mordred was just the latest.

In the end, he only said, "I just wish you could've seen more of his painting. That's all."

The soldier's friend remarked on another rumor he heard. That Arthur was not really dead. God had turned him into a bird, and he had flown away, back to the secret world beyond the mists.

The soldier wondered, privately, if God had been kind enough to let Mordred fly away, too.

IGRAINE, QUEEN OF SPADES

THE CAPTIVE QUEEN

Even when Igraine was very young, she knew of her mother's great power, and so she understood that her life had not been made for herself alone but for her mother's purposes. She made sure to seem polite, and always appeared to obey. But inside, she was looking for an escape route.

Igraine refused her mother's offer to teach her magic, not wishing to be molded in her image. But later, she learned that her mother had never wanted Igraine to learn, and knew that her encouragement would be the quickest deterrent for a contrary daughter.

Later, when she was sent away to be married, Igraine was relieved. Finally, she was far away, outside of her mother's line of sight. But her new husband's kingdom was vital in its influence over the neighboring islands, and Igraine felt that she had been used as her mother's pawn after all.

Then she met Uther, and thought she had found a chance at real escape. Uther was everything her cold, cruel husband was not. He was brave and kind, and had claim to the throne not just of some island but of all Britain. He wanted to take her away and make her his Queen.

That fateful night, when he came to her in disguise to spirit her away, they walked down to the shore to wait for his boat, and doubt crept into her mind again. Had her mother sent her to an unbearably loveless marriage on purpose, so she would throw herself into Uther's arms without question?

The possibilities were endless, dizzying. But then Uther called to her from waist deep in the warm waves. He was smiling. His beautiful hair shone in the starlight. The soft water lapped against his strong, dark body. His eyes seemed to truly see her—as a person and friend, not a queen or a conquest—and loved her in a way she had never known before.

Even if this were all her mother's plan, she realized she didn't care. She might even have cause to thank her. Igraine waded into the water, not minding if her dress got wet, and at last let herself go into his arms.

AGRAVAIN,
JACK OF CLUBS

THE MIRACLE OF THE UNICORN

The four brothers Gawain, Gaheris, Gareth, and Agravain searched for the unicorn long into the night. It was Agravain who found it at last. It glowed like milky starlight in the soft dark.

It was pretty and quiet as a lake, and all it did was look at him. That gaze burned a hole deep into his core. The unicorn did not harm him. It just looked. Most animals lived in fear of humans, but the unicorn was calm, and the gentle silence in its little patch of meadow was deafening. Why didn't it run? Was it blind, or just stupid? Did it pity Agravain for being so wholly inferior, daring to imagine himself a threat to such a sacred creature? That must be it. That was always it.

Why, he thought, did Mother even want this wretched thing? Just because it was beautiful and lucky enough to be born so? Why should it be special and dear to her heart? Why should she talk so often about how much she would like a unicorn, when he couldn't remember the last time she had so much as spoken his name out loud?

What was so amazing about it? Agravain was looking right at it, and he couldn't see. It was just another filthy stupid animal. Without that horn, it was nothing more than a donkey. Or a calf for slaughter.

He drew his sword. His brothers gasped but didn't move. Mother wanted this creature so badly? He would be a good son and bring her its head.

UTHER PENDRAGON, ACE OF SPADES

THE PROPHECY OF MERLIN

When Queen Igraine was pregnant, Merlin came at midnight to counsel with her and the King. Their son, he said, should be sent away to be fostered by another, or else he would surely be the target of assassins, and he was too important to lose. Uther was glad to hear that his son would be "important," though he wasn't sure what Merlin meant.

"Well, you know," the old man said. "They do say the act of observing changes that which is being observed. So it's hard to say for sure."

Uther still did not know what Merlin was talking about, but he had a certain respect for magical ways, so he kept silent.

Merlin paused. His eyes were alive and intent, as if he were actively listening to some other voice. At last he said, "We believe he will try to bring peace and true equality to the entire world.... And he will fail. Quite miserably."

Uther frowned. "But then, perhaps after he is gone, he will inspire his son or daughter and they will succeed? Or, he will inspire others?"

"Yes, he will inspire many others. They will all fail. No one succeeds. At least, not as far as I have seen. Though, again, the observer effect."

In his rambling way, Merlin said that no person would ever achieve Arthur's goal of peace for the world. And Merlin's sight had quite a far reach. Centuries, on and on...

Uther felt a stabbing pang of despair. "Don't taunt us, wizard. Why do you say my son is important, then say that not only will he fail to bring peace, but all of humanity will fail, forever into the future? If that's true, why should we even . . . What is the point of it all?"

"I don't know, my King. Your son will try and fail—is that important? Is there any worth at all just in trying?"

And with a jolt of fear, Uther realized the question was not rhetorical. The old man was just as afraid as he was. He truly did not know the answer.

Uther did what he always did when he wasn't certain, and turned to his wife.

"Of course it is worth it to try," she said. "And I don't ever want to hear you ask that again."

The King nodded, assured. Merlin smiled. It was hard to tell if he had been convinced. But he thanked them both, shook their hands, and turned away without another word. Then, under the quiet light of the full moon, he was gone.

YVAIN, JACK OF DIAMONDS

THE KNIGHT OF THE LION

Morgan used to take her son walking in the misty morning before the rest of the kingdom woke. She told him stories, the kind that had magic and faeries in them. He never once doubted that they were true.

"You are descended from a long line of magic, my dear," she told him. "As I was. And people will want to use you for that magic, but they will also fear you for it. Ever since I was born, my own mother sought to use me for her own secret purposes, and I swear I will never burden you with such a fate."

She told him to keep the magic in his blood a secret and to go out in the world and never let anyone be his keeper—not even her. Yvain didn't understand, but he loved her, so he promised.

Yvain grew into a fine young knight, celebrated by the whole of Camelot. His most famous deed was to spare the life of a fearsome lion, who loved him ever after. Not since Lancelot and Gawain was a knight so respected and adored.

He held up his promise to his mother, and kept the secret of his magic blood hidden. Thankfully, he had just enough of a gift to save him from being lonely.

In the misty mornings, when they had a chance to walk together alone, Yvain told the old faerie stories to his friend the lion, and the lion whispered back, in a soft growl, with stories of his own.

CARD GAMES

✦ ✦ ✦

ALUETTE

✦

This is an old French game, and a favorite of Lancelot's (who hails from France). He introduced it to the Round Table, and it quickly became popular among the knights. Even the King and Queen joined in. This game may be played with two players, if you are wanting for participants. However, it is truly meant to be played with four players, in teams of two, with each team competing against the other.

The funny thing is, the Queen usually ends up playing on Lancelot's team instead of her husband's. Perhaps she feels that a team of royalty would have an unfair advantage against the humble knights . . . ?

Setup

This game is usually played with a Spanish-style deck, which has fewer cards than the one we have. However, you can simulate this by removing the 10 of each suit from the deck. Once you have done so, you're ready to play.

Once the players decide on teams, nine cards from the shortened deck are dealt to each player.

The player to the left of the dealer puts down the first card, and the other players follow with their own cards. When each player has put down a card, the "trick" is complete. The player who has put down the highest-ranked card wins the trick. They take the cards they have won and place them in a face-down pile near them, and may only look at the cards again once the hand is over and it's time to see who the winner is.

When the next trick starts, the first player becomes the dealer, and the player to their left plays the first card, and so forth.

You should know that in Aluette, the cards are ranked differently than they usually are in other games. They are ranked as follows:

"**Luettes**" are the highest rank. These are (in order from highest to lowest) the 3 of Clubs, the 3 of Hearts, the 2 of Clubs, and the 2 of Hearts.

"**Doubles**" are the second highest rank. They are, in order, the 9 of Hearts, the 9 of Clubs, the 2 of Diamonds, and the 2 of Spades.

"**Figures**" are the third highest rank. They are the Kings, Queens, and Jacks, in that order, regardless of suit.

"**Bigailles**" are the lowest rank. They are all of the remaining cards of each suit that were not specifically named previously, in the following order: 9, 8, 7, 6, 5, 4, 3, and 2.

If two cards of equal rank are played, the one following the suit of the first card played wins the trick. For example, if the first player plays the 7 of Clubs and two others play the King of Clubs and King of Diamonds, the King of Clubs would take the trick, assuming that King was the highest rank played.

The "hand" is complete when all nine cards from each participant has been played. After that, nine new cards are dealt to each player to start a new hand. The first player, or team, to win twelve hands wins the game!

Usually the winner of a hand is the player or team who has won the most tricks, but there are some special exceptions:

If a player wins a trick that contains the **3 of Diamonds**, they win the whole hand, even if they did not win the most tricks.

A player who wins a trick containing the **Jack of Spades (Mordred)** loses the whole hand, even if they won the most tricks.

If neither the **3 of Diamonds** nor **Mordred** shows up in any player's hand, the winner is simply the **person who has won the most tricks**.

Easy enough!

Now remember, Aluette is meant to be played in teams of two. That means, if your partner wins more tricks, you are winning, too. "Table talk," or verbal discussion between teammates, is against the rules during Aluette (not to mention poor strategy, as speaking aloud will alert your opponents to your plans). However, hand signals and other visual cues (like winking) are encouraged as part of the fun. Lancelot and Guinevere have a special series of hand signals they use during Aluette. I wonder when they had time to come up with that? Perhaps you and your partner can come up with some, too. Enjoy yourselves!

KARNÖFFEL

✦

This is quite a popular game around the Round Table. With my future sight, I know that in your time, it is considered the oldest known game played with a traditional deck of cards. But to Arthur and his companions, it is just a good time.

Karnöffel is similar to Aluette in that it is a trick-taking game, although the rules can be a bit more complicated. It can be played one-on-one, or with up to eight players (so it is good for large parties). Like in Aluette, the deck must be modified in order to play Karnöffel. Simply remove the Aces of each suit, and you are ready to play.

Begin by dealing five cards to each player, one at a time. The first card dealt to each player must be played face up, and the rest face down. Once all cards for the round are dealt, the lowest-ranking face up card will determine the "trump suit," or the winning suit for the round. (I will explain the rankings in detail a little later.) An interesting thing about Karnöffel is the players are free to look at their face down cards once they have been dealt and decide if they want to give up on the hand or not. Of course this means they will automatically lose the hand, but perhaps they see this as a foregone conclusion anyway and are willing to wait until the next hand to try again.

Once the trump suit is determined, the players gather up their five-card hands and begin the round. The player to the left of the dealer begins by leading with their first card. Then each player plays their own card. The cards do not have to follow the trump suit, or the suit led by the first player. However, the highest ranked card of the leading suit wins the trick, unless a high-ranking card of the "trump suit" was played instead. (Again, I will explain in detail a little later.)

Once each participant has played one card, the player with the highest-ranked card wins the trick, and leads the next card. The round continues until one player has won three tricks (or has the most tricks after all the cards have been played). That player is considered the winner of the round and may begin the next round. Play as many rounds as you like! Around the Table, we like to play at least five.

The **rankings of the cards** are as follows:

The highest-ranked card you can play is the **Jack of the trump suit**, which is determined at the start of the round. This card is called the "**Karnöffel**." Playing the Karnöffel beats any other card, no matter what. That means that depending on what suit was chosen at the beginning, your most valuable card is either Galahad, Mordred, Yvain, or Agravain.

The next-highest rank is the **7 of the trump suit**, which is also known as the "**Devil**." It beats every other card, except for the Karnöffel, as long as it is the **first card played in a trick**. Otherwise, it **loses to every other card**. Also keep in mind that the **"Devil" cannot be played in the first trick**. In other words, it is a powerful card, but only if you know how to use it.

Next is the **6 of the trump suit**, also called the "**Pope**." It beats all cards except for the Karnöffel and the Devil.

Following that is the **2 of the trump suit**, also called the "**Emperor**." It beats all but the Karnöffel, Devil, and Pope.

The **3 of the trump suit** beats any card except the Karnöffel, Devil, Pope, Emperor, or the King of any suit.

The **4 of the trump suit** beats any card except the Karnöffel, Devil, Pope, and Emperor, or the King and Queen of any suit.

The **5 of the trump suit** beats any card except the Karnöffel, Devil, Pope, and Emperor, or the face card of any other suit.

(Complicated, isn't it? Feel free to keep this book open while you're playing, for reference. Don't worry, you'll get the hang of it soon enough.)

Finally, all the other cards are ranked as follows, in order from highest to lowest: **King**, **Queen**, **Jack**, **10**, **9**, **8**, **7**, **6**, **5**, **4**, **3**, and **2**. If none of the trump cards listed above have been played, the winner is the highest-ranked card of the same suit as the first card that was played.

So, for example, if the first player leads with Diamonds, and the trump suit is Clubs, a King of Diamonds would be the highest card you could play, if you don't have any cards in the trump suit.

Though it may seem complicated, while playing Karnöffel you might see similarities with many modern games you play today, like hearts or even poker. And remember, when you play a card game that is hundreds of years old, you are keeping its history alive. When I think about the future, I know that Arthur and his friends are long gone, but we can still play the same games they loved, and pass the time in the same ways they did. As long as you have a deck of cards, this part of history is also part of you.

CARTOMANCY

✦

A Note from Merlin:

Keep in mind that the only true way to tell the future is to be a great wizard like myself, who was born with the gift of the Second Sight. Perhaps you already have some degree of magical ability yourself, but whether you do, or do not, there isn't much I can do to teach you that particular gift. However, I do find that little fortune-telling games like this are good fun, even if you can't really use them to see the future. Games like this are simply what we make of them, which is the same thing you can say about the future itself, so perhaps there is something real to them after all.

Cartomancy—the art of fortune-telling with simple playing cards—is quite straightforward. Simply lay out your deck in a calm, soothing space. Clear your mind, shuffle the cards, spread them out, and choose whichever one your hand is drawn to. Use the guide on the following pages to see what your card means for you. Feel free to try it on your friends, too. —Merlin

Ace of Hearts: Something new and strange will come into your life, for good or ill.

2 of Hearts: You will be lucky in love!

3 of Hearts: You should be wary of love.

4 of Hearts: It's time to travel to a new place.

5 of Hearts: Someone you know is jealous of you.

6 of Hearts: New love will come into your life.

7 of Hearts: A promise will be broken.

8 of Hearts: You are due for a surprising visitor.

9 of Hearts: A wish you made will come true.

10 of Hearts: Good fortune will come to you.

Jack of Hearts: You will meet a youth who means well, but be careful—we all know what they say about good intentions.

Queen of Hearts: You will meet a sweet and kindly woman who will try to soothe your pain.

King of Hearts: You will meet a man who can help you, if only you know the right way to ask.

Ace of Spades: Something in your life will meet an unlucky ending. Hopefully it isn't something of great importance.

2 of Spades: You will have to make a difficult decision.

3 of Spades: Someone you love is not being honest.

4 of Spades: Beware of illness.

5 of Spades: You will succeed, though it will be very difficult.

6 of Spades: Take the small victories where you can get them.

7 of Spades: Beware givers of bad advice. (Not from me, of course.)

8 of Spades: Danger is closer than you think— be careful.

9 of Spades: Sadness and worry cloud your judgment.

10 of Spades: You are trapped in some way and seek freedom.

Jack of Spades: You will meet an immature and unpleasant youth. Avoid them if you can.

Queen of Spades: You will meet a widow, and won't be sure if she needs your help.

King of Spades: You will meet an ambitious man, who, despite his success, seems sad.

Ace of Clubs: Great personal gain and fortune will soon come to you. Enjoy it—the stars don't align like this for just anyone.

2 of Clubs: Someone is gossiping about you.

3 of Clubs: Great wealth will come to someone you love.

4 of Clubs: A friend may be ready to betray you, though it may not be as dramatic as it sounds.

5 of Clubs: A new friend is on the horizon.

6 of Clubs: Money is coming your way.

7 of Clubs: Success in your career will come, but at the cost of your personal life.

8 of Clubs: You will have troubles with both money and love.

9 of Clubs: Avoid being stubborn—instead, embrace change.

10 of Clubs: You will go on an unexpected journey and find fortune.

Jack of Clubs: You will find a friend who will be loyal no matter what, though sometimes it is better to have a friend who can stand up to you.

Queen of Clubs: You will meet a confident older woman, and you will find that she does not need you at all.

King of Clubs: You will meet a very strong man, yet somehow, you will not envy the strength he has.

Ace of Diamonds: A wonderful gift will lift your spirits. Material things aren't everything, but they are very nice to have, once in a while.

2 of Diamonds: Someone in your life will have a relationship you disapprove of.

3 of Diamonds: Look out—you have legal troubles in your future.

4 of Diamonds: You will come into a surprising inheritance.

5 of Diamonds: You will be very happy both at home and at work. Lucky you!

6 of Diamonds: Troubles with your relationship abound. It's up to you whether you want to stay the course.

7 of Diamonds: Things are becoming difficult with your work.

8 of Diamonds: Things are quiet now, but later in your life, you will have a surprising adventure.

9 of Diamonds: You will find a new career opportunity that you never expected.

10 of Diamonds: You will have great wealth and good luck.

Jack of Diamonds: You will meet an interesting, yet unreliable, young person. If you're okay with taking chances, follow them.

Queen of Diamonds: You will meet a flirtatious young woman. Whether this is good luck, or bad, depends on your point of view.

King of Diamonds: You will meet a truly wonderful man, the greatest wizard of all time, beloved by all. Your life will be improved immeasurably by meeting this amazing scholar of magic. (Haha, just my little joke.)

REX QUONDAM REX QUE FUTURUS

CONCLUSION

✦

So, now that you have read Arthur's stories and played his games, I'm sure you are wondering: Is it all real? Do these words tell the truth of him? Are these the games he really played with his companions? Having known him, I should be able to answer that with some certainty, but my memory is a strange thing these days. I will say this: I believe that there are pieces of truth to be found here, and that many things can be true at the same time—this, I think, is the very foundation of magic. There is something magic, too, about playing with cards. Though many other people may have cards that look like yours, your deck becomes your own, worn and soft by years of playing, and the faces on them become as known to you as friends. They become your own knights, your own companions. Read Arthur's stories, play his games—the truth of his life will live in you as it does in me. —Merlin

ACKNOWLEDGMENTS

✦

MAGNOLIA PORTER SIDDELL

Thank you first and foremost to Ver, for taking on this project with me and elevating it beyond my wildest dreams. To my agent Susan and to Katie Gould, for their tireless help to make it a reality. As always, to my husband, Tom, and my son, Nate, for their endless love and support. And to the late T. H. White, the author who lit a fire in my mind.

BIBLIOGRAPHY & FURTHER READING

♦

Le Morte D'Arthur. Thomas Malory, written in 1485, modern edition published March 24, 2011. Considered the foundation of modern Arthur text as we know it.

The Once and Future King and *The Book of Merlyn.* T. H. White, published in 1958 and 1977, from material written between 1938 and 1940. An emotional and philosophical retelling that tragically contextualizes the story with World War II and the rise of Hitler.

The Mists of Avalon. Marion Zimmer Bradley, published 1983. A feminist retelling that centered the women of the story and the Celtic origins of the legend before it was Christianized.

Gawain and the Green Knight. Fourteenth-century poem by unknown author, translated by J. R. R. Tolkien to be published in 1925. One of the most well-known Arthur stories and a good example of how the older Arthurian tales were recontextualized from earlier versions to center Christianity and the values of chivalry.

The History of Merlin and King Arthur. Geoffrey of Monmouth. Originally written in 1136 AD, translated in 1718 by Arthur Thompson, and revised and corrected by J. A. Giles in 1842. The earliest known account of King Arthur in written text.

The Death of King Arthur. A celebrated fifteenth-century alliterative poem by an unknown author, with a new verse translation by Simon Armitage published in 2012.

King Arthur in Legend and History. Richard White, originally published in 1815. A comprehensive illustrated guide to various Arthurian stories and legends, with context to explain their historical continuity